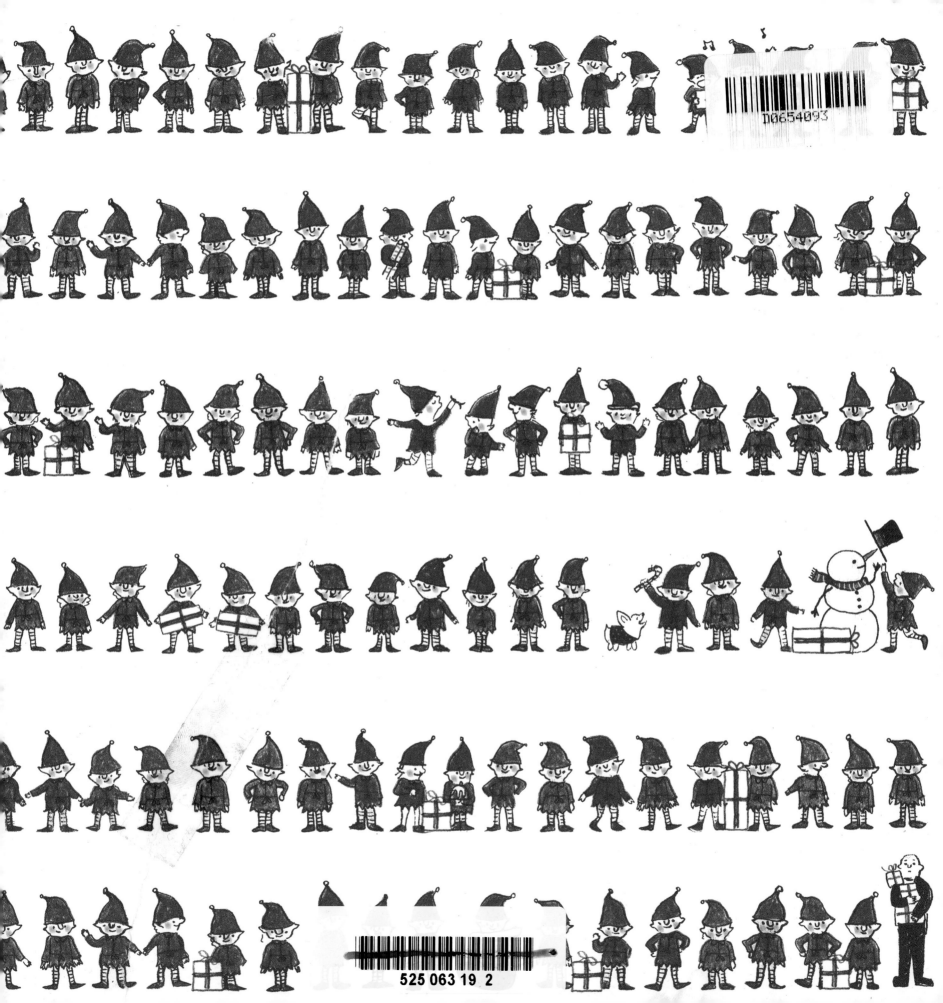

THE QUEEN'S PRESENT

Steve Antony

To Kiki and Kathryn

HODDER CHILDREN'S BOOKS
First published in Great Britain in 2016 by Hodder and Stoughton

Text and illustrations copyright © Steve Antony, 2016

A CIP catalogue record of this book
is available from the British Library.

ISBN: 978 1 444 92563 0

10 9 8 7 6 5 4 3 2 1

Printed and bound in China.

Hodder Children's Books
An imprint of
Hachette Children's Group
Part of Hodder and Stoughton
Carmelite House
50 Victoria Embankment
London EC4Y 0DZ

An Hachette UK Company
www.hachette.co.uk

www.hachettechildrens.co.uk

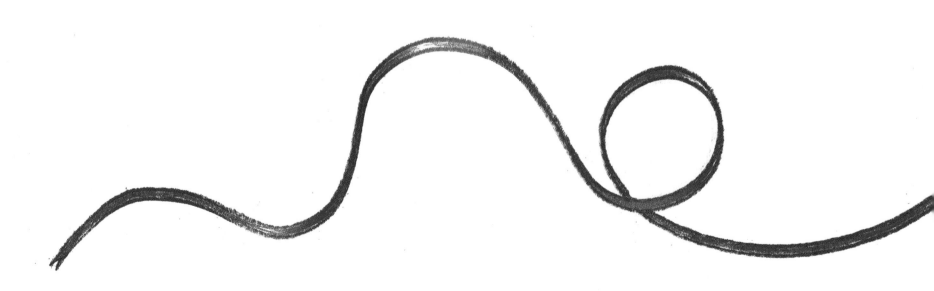

THE QUEEN'S PRESENT

Steve Antony

Hodder
Children's
Books

It was **Christmas Eve** and the Queen still hadn't found the perfect present for the little prince and princess.

Luckily, someone special was
just around the corner to help...

Ho ho ho!

Father Christmas flew down the street and in a whistle they were off...

around the world in search
of the perfect present!

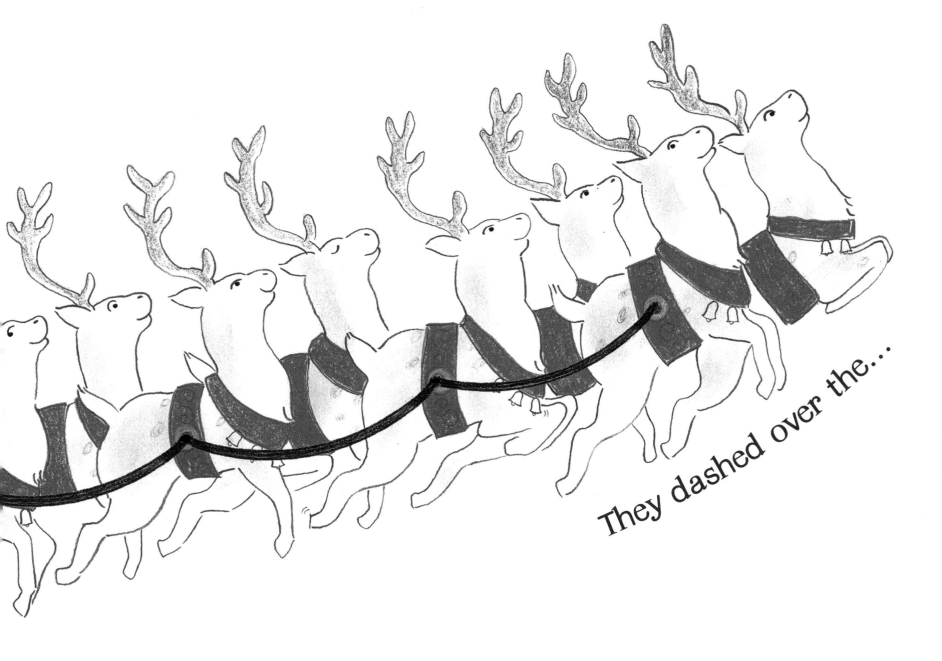

They dashed over the...

Eiffel Tower in Paris.

They pranced around the...

Leaning Tower of Pisa.

They soared up to the...

Great Pyramids of Egypt.

They glided along the...

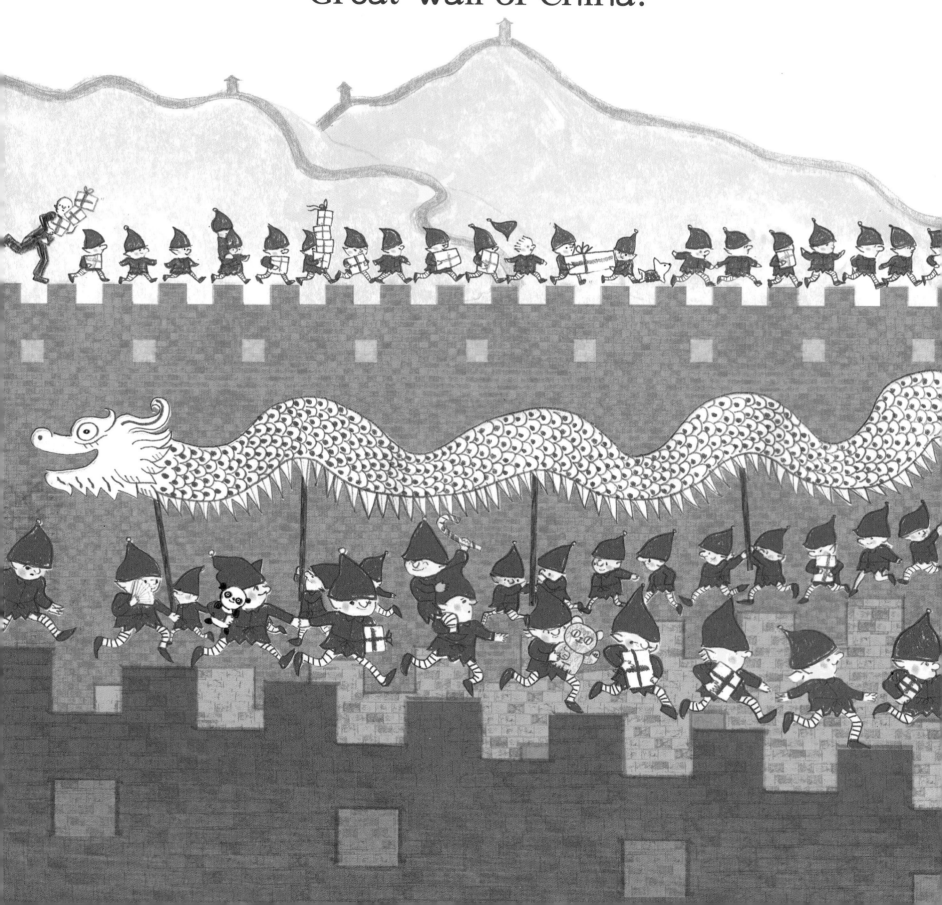

Great Wall of China.

They darted past the...

Himeji Castle in Japan.

They swooped to the...

Sydney Opera House
in Australia.

They flew over the...

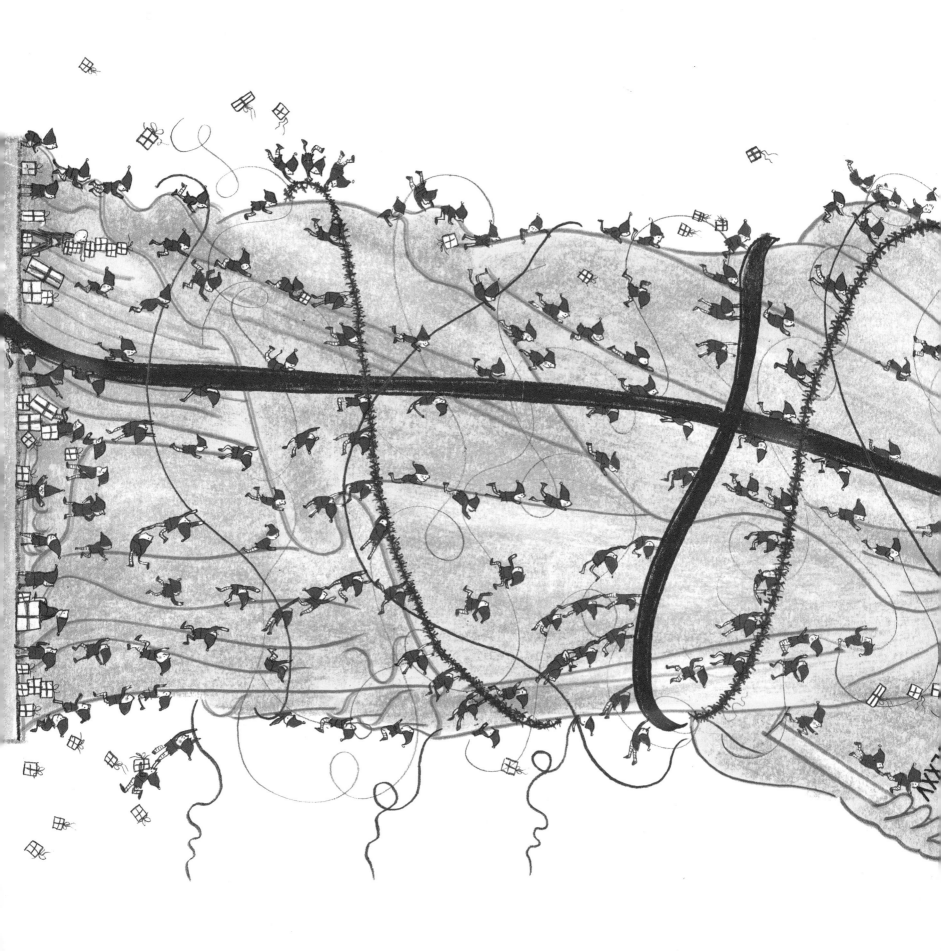

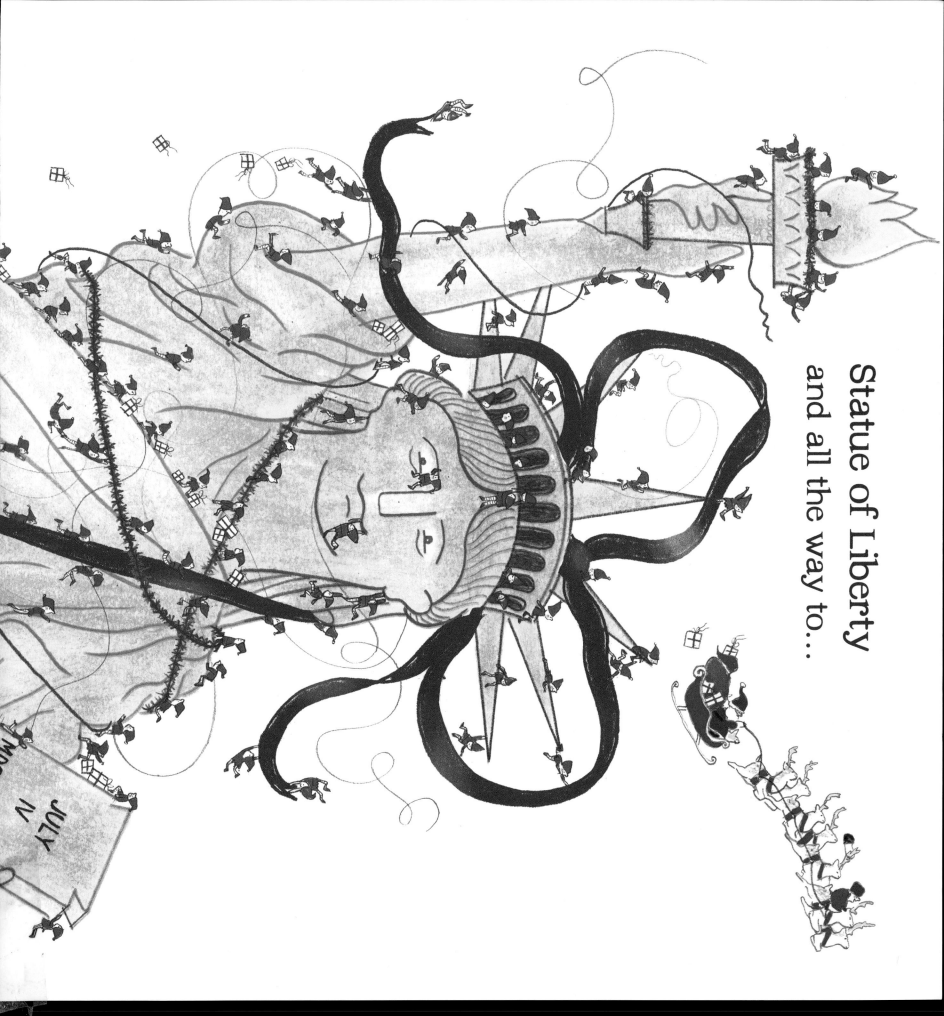

Statue of Liberty
and all the way to...

The North Pole,

but they still couldn't find the perfect present.

It was nearly Christmas Day so Father
Christmas took the Queen home to...

Sandringham House in England,

where the little prince and princess
received the best present of all...